The WOBBLYSAURUS

For Grandma G, Nanny S & Grandad C, Grandma P
& Grandad K. Thank you for always being
there for my little Wobblysauruses.
R.B.

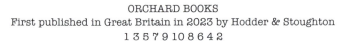

ORCHARD BOOKS
First published in Great Britain in 2023 by Hodder & Stoughton
1 3 5 7 9 10 8 6 4 2

Text © Rachel Bright 2023
Illustrations © Chris Chatterton 2023

HB ISBN 978 1 40835 618 0
PB ISBN 978 1 40835 619 7

Printed and bound in China

MIX
Paper from
responsible sources
FSC
www.fsc.org
FSC® C104740

Orchard Books
An imprint of Hachette Children's Group
Part of Hodder & Stoughton Limited
Carmelite House
50 Victoria Embankment
London EC4Y 0DZ

An Hachette UK Company
www.hachette.co.uk
www.hachettechildrens.co.uk

RACHEL BRIGHT   CHRIS CHATTERTON

The
WOBBLYSAURUS

On a dusty, twisty track that
zig-zagged through a bumpy hollow,
A little Wobblysaurus did a
BIG and **GULPY** swallow.

Since later on that afternoon
a BIG event was planned,
When many two-wheeled dinosaurs
would gather on the sand.

BIG
BICYCLE DAY
★ DINO RACE FUN ★

And as she clambered on her bike,
(brand new and shiny red),
An exciting little daydream
went rolling through her head.

She imagined how she'd **ZOOM** *so fast*
upon those speedy pedals,

Impressing every dino there
and winning **ALL** the medals!

But *also* Wobblysaurus had
a tummy full of FLITTERS...
Riding bikes was new to her and
gave her nervous jitters.

So she thought she
ought to practise,
With a dinging of
her bell,

She was off! Hooray!

But OH!

She WIBBLED...

...and she fell!

SCRAPE and

BUMP and

OUCH and

OOPS...
she landed in a heap.

Perhaps for her **FIRST** try that
hill had been a *little* steep.
So she dusted off and climbed
back on to have another go,

This time she'd start out on the flat
and keep it nice and slow . . .

But . . .

"ARGH!"

and, "OH!"

and, "OOOF!"

and, "NO!"

She KEPT on falling down!

Her face had gone from hopeful to a rather brooding frown.

She tried SO many times and then she *even* tried some MORE.

She tried until she couldn't and her bottom was quite sore!

She fought to hold back
stinging tears that
welled up in her eyes,
But just when all
seemed hopeless,
she was in for a
SURPRISE ...

From up upon the hill

there came a loud and happy yell,

"WOO-HOO! YOO-HOO!"

It was a voice she knew extremely well!

Her **GRANNYSAUR** came speeding
down to wipe her salty tears,
And give her some advice about her
riding hopes and fears.

"My lovely Wobblysaurus,
I want to tell a tale
Of another Wibblysaurus
who *often* used to fail!

No matter what she tried, she couldn't ride *at all*, you see.

And that little Wibblysaurus?
Well, my darling . . .

. . . she was **ME!**"

RUNNER UP

1st

First

Then Granny showed her pictures
of when she was quite small.
She'd tumbled, flipped and crashed and bumped!
Had **EVERY** kind of fall!

But slow and sure and day-by-day,
she'd mastered how to ride,

And **NOW** she was a legend!
Famous far and wide!

"You see," said Granny gently,
"all the BEST things take a while,
And we're all on one big journey,
NOT a race!" she wisely smiled.

"I think, in life, it's not about how
fast we ride the track,
But more that when we fall,
we find a way to bounce right back.

And something I have noticed
– *your* very special thing –
Is you are full of DON'T-GIVE-UPS
and I-can-do-it ZING!"

Then Wobblysaurus saw herself
in quite a different light,
And trying with some wobbling ...
well ... now it felt alright!

So Grannysaur taught Wobblysaur
some nifty little tricks,
And Wobblysaur had good ideas
to throw into the mix!

"The race is nearly starting!
Let's do this as a team!"
"Yes!" cried Wobblysaurus,
"that's even *better* than my dream!"

And that year's Biking Fun-Day
had some tandem racing too,
And **EVERYONE** found something
that they really liked to do.

And all the dinos, big and small,
they came to join the fun,
They rode around together in the
setting evening sun.

So whatever you are learning and
whatever's feeling TOUGH,
Just remember you'll be looking back
(one day) at all that stuff,

Telling tales of times you tried
SO hard at something new,
And then, one happy, special day . . .

...you found your wheels and FLEW!

HOORAY!